EPILEPSY

Published by Smart Apple Media
1980 Lookout Drive
North Mankato, Minnesota 56003

Copyright © 2001 Smart Apple Media.
International copyrights reserved in all countries.
No part of this book may be reproduced in any form without
written permission from the publisher.
Printed in the United States of America.

Photos: page 7—Michael Freeman/CORBIS; page 10—Indexstock:
BSIP Agency; page 11—Hulton-Deutsch Collection/CORBIS;
page 12—LifeART, Lippincott Williams & Wilkins; pages 20,
21—CORBIS; page 25—Robert Maass/CORBIS; page 29—Pascal
Rondeau /Allsport

Design and Production: EvansDay Design

Library of Congress Cataloging-in-Publication Data

Vander Hook, Sue, 1949–
Epilepsy / by Sue Vander Hook
p. cm. – (Understanding illness)
Includes index.
Summary: Describes the nature, symptoms, and possible causes
of epilepsy, a history of its study, and its treatment.
ISBN 1-58340-025-7
1. Epilepsy—Juvenile literature. [1. Epilepsy. 2. Diseases.] I.
Title. II. Series: Understanding illness (Mankato, Minn.)

RC372.V36   2000
616.8'53—dc21   99-39170

First edition

9 8 7 6 5 4 3 2 1

EPILEPSY

Sue Vander Hook

A *stone* TOSSED INTO

CREATES A SMALL SPLASH THAT GROWS TO

MANY EXPANDING RIPPLES. THE SAME TYPE OF EFFECT IS CAUSED BY THE BRAIN DISORDER KNOWN AS EPILEPSY. THE HUMAN BRAIN HAS BILLIONS OF CELLS CALLED NEURONS THAT SEND AND RECEIVE ELECTRICAL SIGNALS BETWEEN THE BRAIN AND THE BODY. SOMETIMES NEURONS SEND OUT TOO MANY ELECTRICAL SIGNALS, WHICH OVERLOAD THE BRAIN AND BODY. THIS ELECTRICAL DISTURBANCE—CALLED A SEIZURE—MAY STAY IN ONE SMALL AREA, OR IT MAY RIPPLE OUTWARD THROUGH THE WHOLE BODY, CAUSING VIOLENT CONVULSIONS.

A CALM POND

UNDERSTANDING
EPILEPSY

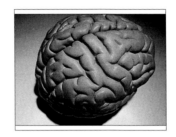

Having one seizure does not necessarily mean that a person has epilepsy. But if a person continues to experience seizures over an extended period of time, he or she probably has the disorder. People with epilepsy may have a seizure only once in a while, or they may have several every day. Almost 2.5 million people in the

Nonstop electrical and chemical activity in the brain is constantly sending messages to the rest of the body.

United States alone have some form of epilepsy, and 30 percent of them are under the age of 18.

In about 75 percent of epilepsy cases, doctors do not know the exact cause of the brain's electrical disturbances. The other 25 percent of cases may be caused by brain damage at birth, severe head injuries, **strokes**, brain tumors, lead poisoning, or drug or alcohol abuse. Infections that affect the brain—such as

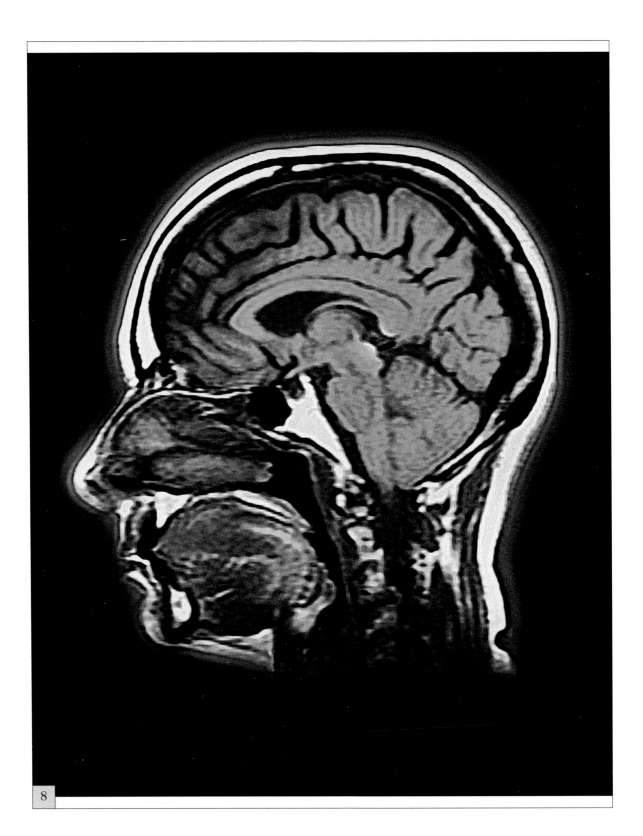

meningitis and **viral encephalitis**—can also lead to epilepsy. Some types of seizures can be genetic. Juvenile Myoclonic Epilepsy (JME) has been traced to a **gene** inherited from a parent.

Epilepsy is divided into categories, each named for the type of seizure it causes. *Petit mal* (which means "small illness") epilepsy, the mildest form of the disorder, affects mainly children. A child with this type of epilepsy may suddenly stop an activity and stare blankly around for a minute or so, unaware of what is happening. These seizures are sometimes called absences.

If a person has temporal lobe epilepsy, he or she may suddenly become violent or angry, laugh for no reason, or make odd chewing motions. Another type, called focal epilepsy, begins with uncontrollable twitching in a small part of the body. The twitching spreads until it

Modern imaging techniques can show doctors what happens in the brain during a seizure.

meningitis: a bacteria-caused inflammation of the thin layer surrounding the brain

viral encephalitis: an inflammation of the brain caused by a virus

gene: a tiny unit that controls which characteristics people inherit from their parents

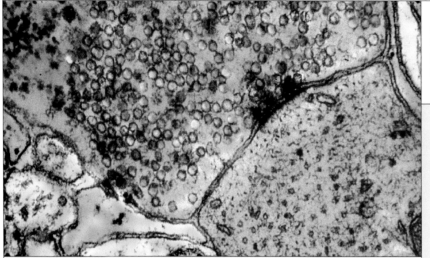

A microscopic view of a neuron. When these cells are not working properly, a person may have one of several types of epilepsy.

Brain scans are critical in the study of epilepsy. They show parts of the brain from all different sides.

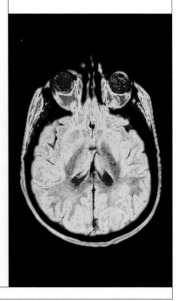

affects the entire body, though the person does not lose consciousness.

A more severe type of epilepsy, called *grand mal* (which means "great illness"), causes people to lose consciousness. Most of these seizures occur without warning. The person's body twitches and jerks uncontrollably, and he or she may vomit or lose bladder control. The seizure may last several minutes and is often followed by a deep sleep or a state of confusion. The seizure itself is not painful; there is usually no danger unless the person falls down. Once neurons stop sending the extra electrical signals, the seizure stops and the brain again functions normally.

In extreme cases, however, a grand mal seizure may become a life-threatening emergency called *status epilepticus*. When this happens, the excessive electrical activity in

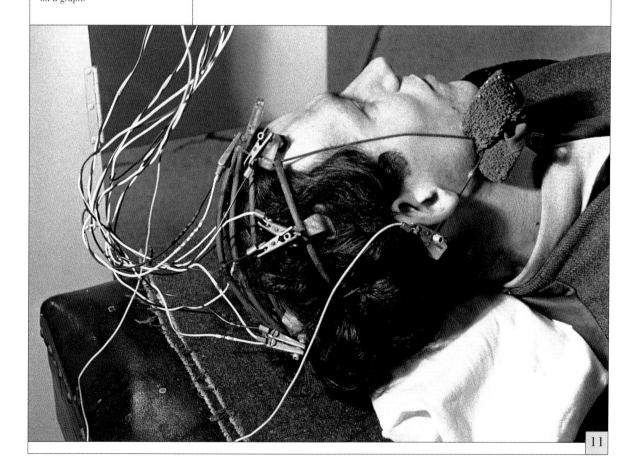

the brain does not stop. One seizure is immediately followed by another. If allowed to continue, the seizures may go on for hours, starving the brain of oxygen and causing brain damage or even death.

Epilepsy is not **contagious**, so there is no danger of "catching" it like a cold. Most people with epilepsy live normal lives, go to school and work, get married, and have children if

contagious: spread from one person to another by contact

The human brain is divided into two halves, connected to the rest of the body by millions of blood vessels and electrical pathways.

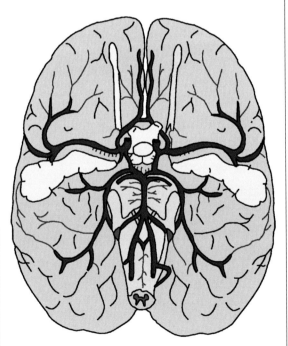

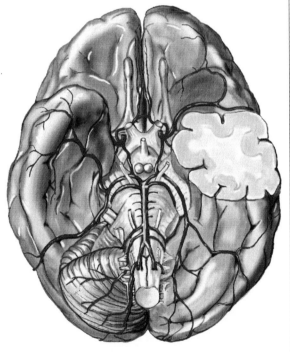

Most epileptics can participate in a wide range of sports, though some activities should be approached with extra caution.

they choose. People whose seizures are under control can drive a car. They can participate in sports, although some contact sports such as boxing may be off-limits. For safety reasons, people with epilepsy, called epileptics, are advised to avoid swimming alone, climbing in high places, or operating dangerous machinery.

Until about 50 years ago, epilepsy was a feared and misunderstood illness with few treatments available.

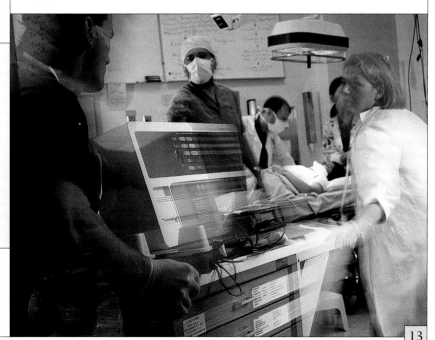

NEW
SOLUTIONS

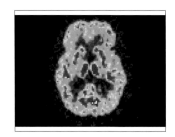

New medical technology continues to improve our methods of studying the brain and its disorders. The electroencephalograph (EEG), whose name means "electric brain writing," is an instrument that records brain waves. Doctors may find special patterns of brain

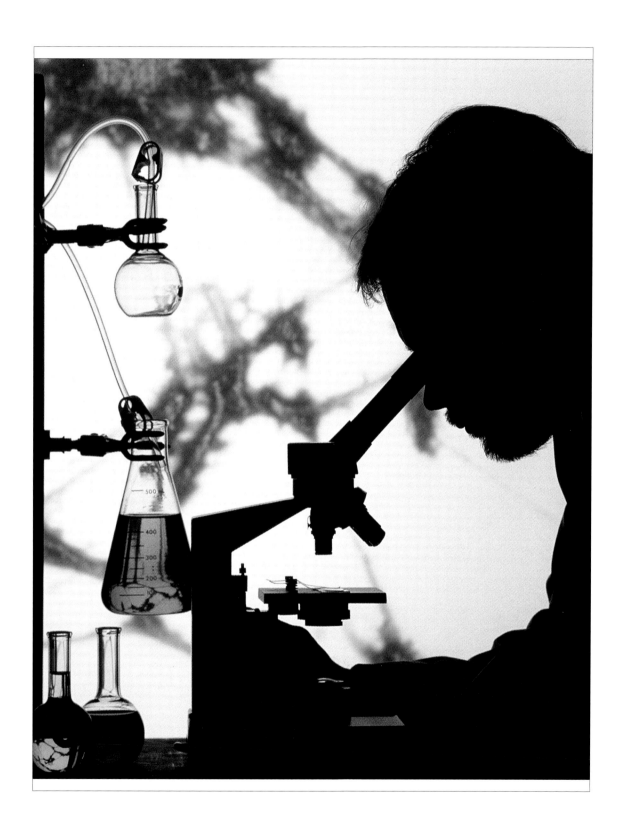

activity during or between seizures that help them decide if a person has epilepsy.

The brain can also be studied using computerized tomography (CT) or magnetic resonance imaging (MRI). Growths, scars, and unusual physical conditions in the brain can be identified with these methods, which allow doctors to look inside a person's skull. Positron-emission tomography (PET) imaging is used in some medical fa-

anticonvulsive: preventing or controlling convulsions

Sophisticated scanning equipment can reveal any unusual conditions or injuries to the brain.

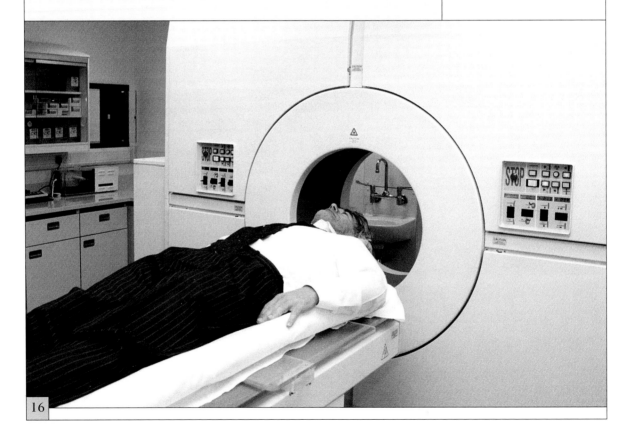

Doctors review the results of a CT scan to learn more about the electrical disturbances in a patient's brain.

cilities to find out which specific area of the brain is causing seizures.

After diagnosis, a doctor must decide on the right treatment to control the seizures. Some patients take **anticonvulsive** or antiepileptic drugs. One type, **barbiturates**, are generally safe, though they may slow learning in children or cause sleepiness. One of the most effective drugs available is phenytoin, commonly known as Dilantin, which was first released in

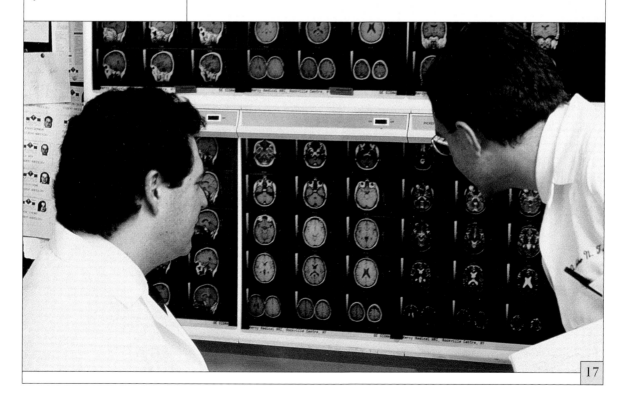

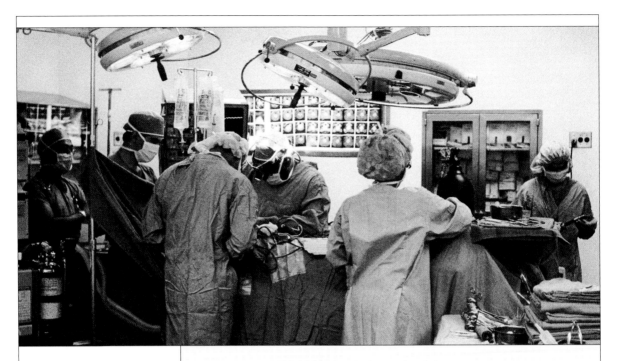

In extreme cases, epilepsy may be treated with surgery. Surgeons may remove a small part of the brain or cut certain nerves.

fasting: to stop eating food for an unusually long time

ketones: poisonous acids produced when the body burns fat for energy

1932. Dilantin is most effective in controlling grand mal seizures.

Another type of epilepsy treatment that has been most successful for children is the ketogenic diet. In ancient times, physicians discovered that **fasting** could help control epileptic seizures. For the first day or two on the ketogenic diet, the child eats no food at all. As the body produces **ketones** during this extreme change, the chemical balance of the blood changes. To keep the blood in this al-

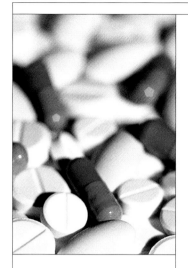

Many epileptics need to take several types of pills every day to control seizures.

carbohydrates: a source of energy found mainly in sugars and starches; one of the three main classes of foods

vagus nerve: a pair of nerves connected directly to the brain; it is linked to the medulla, a part of the brain that controls many of the body's automatic functions

Special diets can sometimes help limit seizures and reduce the need for medication.

tered state, the child then eats foods high in fat and low in **carbohydrates**, as well as a limited amount of calories and no sugar. This diet can decrease and even control seizures in some people.

When other seizure treatments fail, **vagus nerve** stimulation may be tried. In this procedure, a doctor surgically implants a battery-powered device about the size of a silver dollar under the patient's collarbone. Wires from the device are looped around the vagus nerve in the neck. The device sends regular

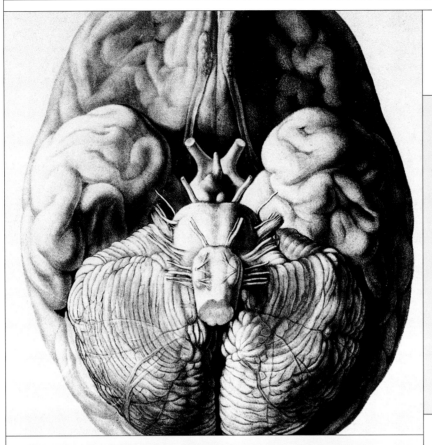

This illustration shows how the human brain is divided into separate but connected lobes.

lobes: rounded parts of an organ of the body, especially the brain or lungs

temporal lobe: part of the brain located at the sides of the head

frontal lobe: part of the brain located at the front of the head

electrical bursts to the brain through the vagus nerve, keeping excessive neuron activity in the brain from growing into a larger disturbance. When electrical currents pass through the nerve, the patient feels a slight tingle and may experience a hoarse voice. This technique can decrease the strength of seizures or completely prevent them in some people.

Advances in medicine continue to make brain surgery a safer and more effective treatment.

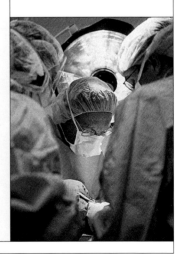

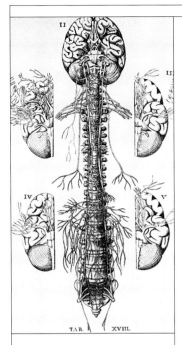

Although epilepsy begins in the brain, its effects may branch out through nerves to impact a person's entire body.

parietal lobe: part of the brain located at the top of the head

occipital lobe: part of the brain located at the back of the head

nerves: bundles of fibers connecting the brain and spinal cord to the rest of the body; they carry electrical impulses between the brain and the body

Surgery is usually the final option in epilepsy treatments. The brain is divided into four **lobes**: the **temporal lobe**, **frontal lobe**, **parietal lobe**, and **occipital lobe**. Various surgeries involve various parts of the brain. A temporal lobectomy is the removal of part or all of the temporal lobe, which is where most seizures originate. A topectomy is the removal of part of the cortex—the outer part of the brain—from the frontal, parietal, or occipital lobes. A corpus callosotomy is a procedure that involves cutting the **nerves** that connect one side of the brain to the other.

Surgery does not guarantee that a person will be free of seizures or won't have to take medicine anymore. But with today's advanced medical technology, surgeries are becoming more and more successful. More people than ever before are able to live full and productive lives with epilepsy.

PARTNERING
TOGETHER

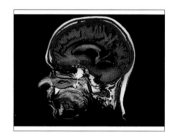

Even though seizures are under control
for about 75 percent of epileptics, the remaining
25 percent should not be forgotten. Epilepsy that does not
respond to treatment affects family life, employment, driving privileges, and relationships with other people. Negative
self-images and fears about an uncertain future can cause

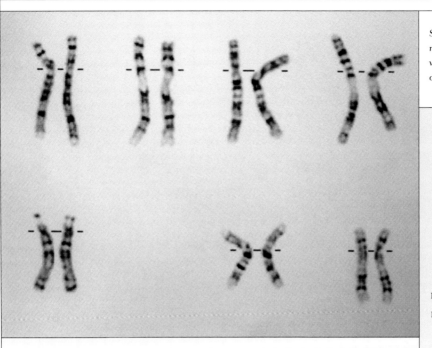

mutated: changed in a major way

depression and other emotional problems. Repeated seizures in children can damage developing brains and result in learning difficulties.

Although scientists and doctors have developed many new ways to study and treat epilepsy, there are still many unanswered questions. Scientists continue to study a **mutated** gene that causes some babies to inherit epilepsy. These infants have seizures until they are about three months old, at which time the seizures stop.

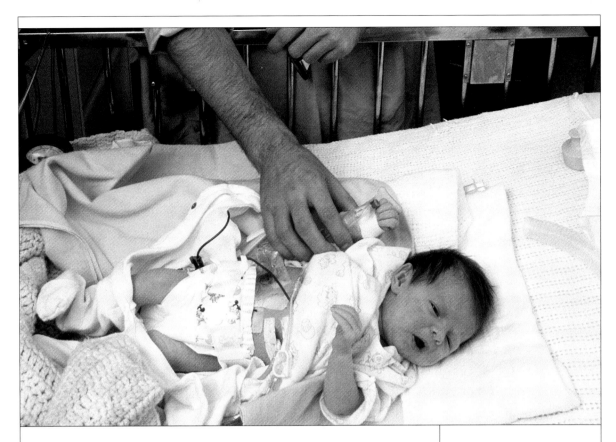

The children often go on to develop epilepsy later in life.

Organizations such as The Epilepsy Foundation, The National Institute of Neurological Disorders and Stroke, and many local and statewide organizations are actively searching for ways to make life better for all people with epilepsy. Their goals are to develop better

Epilepsy may affect people of all races at any stage of life. Some babies are born with the disorder.

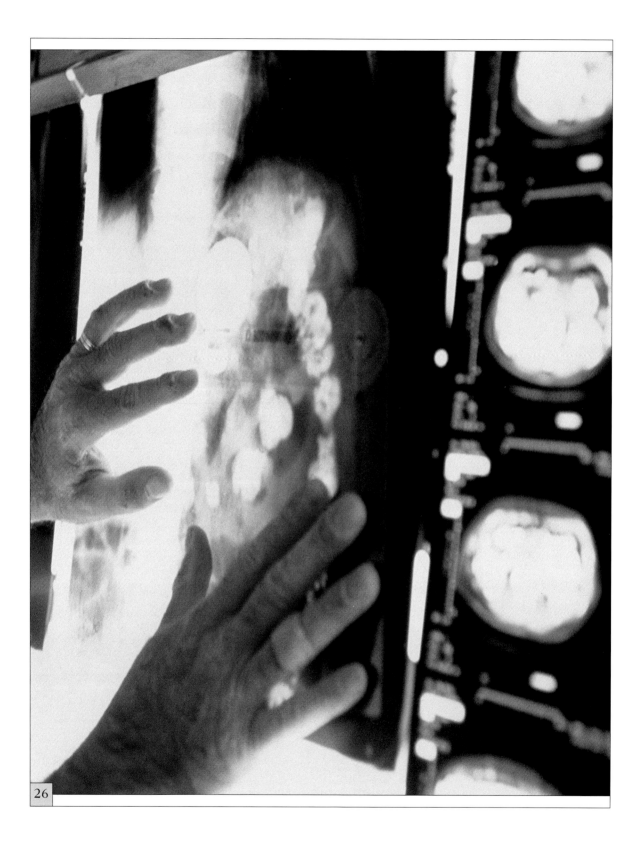

treatments, to educate people on the causes and effects of epilepsy, and to find ways to prevent seizures of all kinds.

It is important to find the physical causes of epilepsy and to develop better treatments. But it is just as important to provide emotional and social support for all people who suffer from epilepsy. With a better understanding of this disorder, we can eliminate old fears and move closer to a cure.

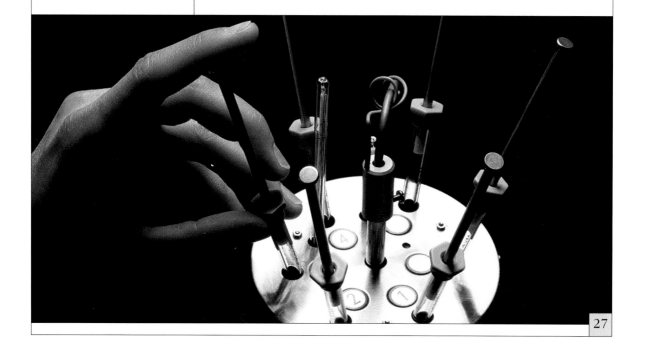

OVERCOMING ILLNESS

MARION CLIGNET
OLYMPIC CYCLIST

"Part of my victory, my second place [finish] today, is over epilepsy." Those were the words of Marion Clignet after winning a silver medal in cycling at the 1996 Summer Olympics in Atlanta, Georgia.

Born in Hyde Park, Illinois, to French parents, Marion had her first seizure while driving a car in 1984 at the age of 21. After being diagnosed with epilepsy, her driver's license was suspended for a year. Forced to find a new way to get to and from work every day, she began riding a bicycle. Before developing epilepsy, Marion had ridden a bicycle only on leisurely outings on neighborhood streets. But after being forced to ride to work every day, she soon developed the urge to bike competitively.

After setting her sights on international competition, Marion began pushing herself hard with strenuous training. Five years

later, she won the women's team 50-kilometer time trial at the U.S. National Cycling Championship. Still, Marion was not satisfied. She felt that the U.S. Cycling Federation did not give her its full support because of her epilepsy. In 1990, Marion decided to continue her cycling pursuits in France by becoming a citizen there. France welcomed her, and in 1991, Marion led the French team to a victory at the world championships.

The 1992 Olympics in Barcelona, Spain, was a disappointment for Marion, who rode with an injury and finished 33rd. Over the next several years, she bounced back with more determination than ever, earning numerous victories and a place on the 1996 Olympic team.

At the Summer Olympics in Atlanta, Marion rode to a silver medal. But her personal victory was even greater. It was a win over epilepsy and a victory for all those who have it. "So many people told me at the beginning, 'Oh, you can't ride because you are an epileptic,'" Marion recalled. "I say, 'Oh, yeah? Watch me.'"

Marion continues to use her standing as one of the best female cyclists in the world to disprove many misunderstandings about epilepsy. She controls her disorder by taking six daily doses of a drug that regulates brain waves. She also continues to help others win their battle against epilepsy through her example of courage and determination.

Epilepsy Education Association, Inc.
4335 1C Irish Hills Drive
South Bend, IN 46614   www.iupui.edu/~epilepsy

The Epilepsy Foundation of America
4351 Garden City Drive
Landover, MD 20785   www.efa.org

The Epilepsy Foundation of Michigan
26211 Central Park Boulevard
Suite 100
Southfield, MI 48076   www.epilepsymichigan.org

Epilepsy Ontario
Suite 308, 1 Promenade Circle
Thornhill, ON L4J 4P8   www.epilepsyontario.org

National Information Center for Children and Youth with Handicaps
P.O. Box 1492
Washington, DC 20013

The National Institute of Neurological Disorders and Stroke
National Institute of Health
U.S. Department of Health and Human Services
Building 31, Room 8A-16
Bethesda, MD 20892   www.ninds.nih.gov